I Said,
"Bed!"

I Said, "Bed!"

by Bruce Degen

I Like to Read®

Holiday House / New York

Copyright © 2014 by Bruce Degen
All Rights Reserved
HOLIDAY HOUSE is registered in the U.S. Patent and Trademark Office.
Printed and Bound in October 2014 at Tien Wah Press, Johor Bahru, Johor, Malaysia.
The artwork was created with colored pencils and graphite pencil on handmade Fabriano Roma
paper with additional lines scratched in with a ca. 1929 Coca-Cola ice pick and bottle opener.
www.holidayhouse.com
3 5 7 9 10 8 6 4 2

Library of Congress Cataloging-in-Publication Data
Degen, Bruce.
I said, "Bed!" / by Bruce Degen.— First edition.
    pages cm. — (I like to read)
Summary: A little boy who is not ready for sleep goes on a bedtime adventure.
ISBN 978-0-8234-2938-7 (hardcover)
[1. Bedtime—Fiction. 2. Imagination—Fiction.] I. Title.
PZ7.D3635Iam 2014
[E]—dc23
2013009568

ISBN 978-0-8234-3311-7 (paperback)

For Chris, who traveled thousands of miles with me in a VW Bug. Maybe not to the moon, but the Grand Tetons and the '68 Chicago Convention were definitely different worlds.